# The Ha

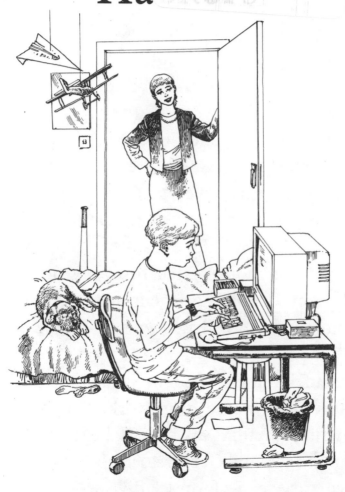

Story by Sandy Lanton

# CHAPTER ONE

"Danny, get up. You'll miss your bus. What did you do? Stay up half the night with your silly computer games? Or were you chatting with your modem friends again? I'm going to shut down your bulletin board if you don't spend some time doing homework."

Danny Hall opened one eye and looked at his mother. She was dressed in her navy blue "executive" suit.

"She's only in stage one," Danny whispered to his dog, Hacker. "She hasn't tapped her foot, started throwing things, called me Daniel, or mentioned my messy room yet." He rolled over to face the wall.

"And I want this room straightened up before I get home from work. How you can find anything in here is beyond me. Daniel, get up! Get dressed. That's if you have any clean clothes left."

"Stage two," whispered Danny.

Mrs. Hall tapped one high-heeled shoe on the floor. "You know I can't drive you to school. Mr. Weber called an emergency staff meeting for this morning. There's no way I can be late with all that's going on at the bank now."

She picked a dirty sock off the stereo, rolled it into a ball, and threw it at Danny.

"Stage three," whispered Danny. He opened his eyes and stroked Hacker's head. Mrs. Hall turned and walked out the door. Danny rolled over and dozed off. About twenty minutes later, the noise of a bunch of kids at the bus stop on the corner woke him. He jumped up and rummaged through the mess on his floor for some clothes. He dressed hurriedly and raced down the steps. Then, grabbing his book bag from the hall and a doughnut from a box on the kitchen table, he ran out the door. He reached the corner just as the bus driver was closing the door. Danny banged on it, and the driver pulled the lever.

"Just in time...again, young Mr. Hall," said the driver, as the bus shuttled off.

"Hey, Dan, what's up?" said Jason, his best friend. "Are you ready for the history test?"

Danny stared blankly. "History test? First period? I forgot all about it."

"It's on chapters 17, 18 and 19," said Jason. "You did read them, didn't you?"

"Yeah, about a week or two ago. I'll probably remember enough to get by. But I better cram a little now."

Danny opened his book and began to read, turning the pages furiously.

Jason turned around in his seat. "Hey, Lauren, have you seen any of the new movies at the Central 12-Plex yet?"

"No," said Lauren.

"Great, then how about going with me tomorrow night?"

"Sure," said Lauren.

"Cool," said Jason. I'll see you around seven."

Lauren gave him a smile. She liked him a lot, and they were good friends.

Ten minutes later the bus lurched to a shuddering stop at Woodvale Middle School. Jason and Lauren walked in together, almost touching hands. Danny followed, still reading his history book.

Danny and Jason went to their lockers. Jason opened his locker, put his jacket away, and took out some books. Danny was turning his combination for the third time when he heard a group of girls going by, chatting and giggling. He recognized one voice as Michelle Matthews. He turned his head to speak, but when he opened his mouth, nothing came out. He cleared his throat and tried again, but still nothing. Just then, his locker opened, and books, sneakers, a football, and assorted junk followed the laws of gravity and almost buried Danny.

Jason cracked up. "Did Juliet go by again?" he asked, helping Danny pick up the stuff.

"How did you guess?" said Danny, putting the rest of the junk back in the locker.

"When are you going to talk to her, Romeo?"

"Soon," said Danny. "One of these days. And stop calling me Romeo." Danny punched his best friend on the arm. "And her name's not Juliet. It's Michelle."

"Listen, Romeo, want to come over after school? We can shoot some hoops and play the new computer game I just got. Maybe you can stay for dinner."

"Sure, I don't feel like cleaning my

room anyway. My mom's working late."

"OK, I'll meet you at the bus. There's the bell. Don't want to keep Ms. Winters waiting."

"Yeah, we might get a COLD reception from Ms. Winters."

"Or the history might get older."

They both laughed as they opened the door to Ms. Winters's room.

## CHAPTER TWO

Elizabeth Hall took a deep breath as she entered the bank's large conference room. Sara Gordon, the bank president's secretary, was already there, setting up for the meeting. She put pads, pencils, and water glasses at each place. She was putting the water pitcher on the table when Mr. Weber, the bank president, entered the room. She picked up a stack of papers from the table and handed them to him.

"I have some letters ready for your signature, Mr. Weber."

Mr. Weber looked past her as he signed the papers.

"Would you make some coffee please, Sara?"

"Yes, Mr. Weber," she said. She walked over to the kitchenette in the corner without looking at him.

"And make it strong. We're going to

need it today. When the staff hears what I have to tell them, we could probably use something stronger than coffee."

"Is there anything I can do?"

"No, just stay and take notes."

Sara Gordon made the coffee and then took her usual place at the table next to Mr. Weber as the rest of the executive staff filed into the room.

"I think some of you may already know why I've called this meeting," Mr. Weber said, pulling his glasses down to the tip of his nose. "The auditors have uncovered a case of embezzlement. Someone has been using our computer system to transfer funds from hundreds of corporations into a dummy corporation. Small amounts were taken from each account, not enough for the individual depositors to notice, but since the bank is responsible, the losses add up to a considerable amount. The total could be in the hundreds of thousands of dollars, perhaps in the millions."

There were murmurs of disbelief from the staff.

"We have to decide on a course of action."

"Have you contacted the police?" asked the Senior Vice President.

"Not yet, Steve. The resulting publicity could lead to panic and a run on the bank. If we can find the thief ourselves, we stand a much better chance of keeping up confidence in our stability."

"Has the thief been attacking individual depositors or companies?" asked another executive.

Mr. Weber looked at his notes. "It's been only large corporations, so far. But we don't know if the thief will expand the operation to attack small accounts as well."

"When have the thefts been occurring?"

asked senior accountant Henry Carter.

Mr. Weber looked at his notes again. "It's been happening on the weekends when the corporate offices were closed, and the accounting department wasn't monitoring their bank transactions."

Elizabeth Hall opened a folder. "I've been going over the figures with the auditors. If these losses continue at the same rate, the bank could go under in a few months, or perhaps weeks, even without a panic by depositors. Have you changed the passwords? It would take a while for the thief to figure them out again."

Mr. Weber took a sip of water before speaking. "No, that would tip our hand. I don't want him to know that we've discovered the theft yet. If we don't have our thief by Monday morning, we'll change our codes and go to the authorities."

Mr. Weber cleared his throat. "I hope I've impressed on you the seriousness of the matter. And remember, if any word of this leaks to the press, I hate to think of the consequences."

He took a watch out of his vest pocket and looked at it. "It's almost nine—time for business. Open the doors, Charlie."

## CHAPTER THREE

As Danny entered the front door of his house, he heard his mother talking on the phone in the kitchen.

"Mr. Weber, I've been thinking about this embezzlement problem all day. I hate to bring up an unpleasant possibility, but it could be an inside job. Perhaps the access codes were stolen by someone inside the bank. If that's the case, the thief already knows we're on to him. I think we should change the codes right now and contact the authorities. I don't think we have a chance of catching him ourselves. Maybe the police can keep a lid on the story until the investigation is completed...All right, I understand. I'll see you in the morning."

Danny walked over to his mother and put his arm around her. "What's up, Mom. I couldn't help overhearing. Is everything OK?"

"Hi, Danny. Did you have a good time at Jason's house? Thanks for calling. I'm glad you're not the kind of kid I have to worry about."

Danny poured two glasses of orange juice and handed one to his mother. "Yeah, it was cool, but stop changing the subject. I know you have something more important on your mind than keeping track of what I'm up to."

"You're right. I do have a lot on my mind. I guess it will help to talk it out. I don't know what I'm going to do. We have to find this embezzler, or the bank will close its doors and lots of people will be out of work...including me.

Danny swallowed a mouthful of juice. "Don't worry, Mom, you're a good executive. You'll find another job."

"I hope it doesn't come to that, Son. I haven't lost my job yet. But this really hurts. I love the bank and the people I work with. I can't believe that any one of them could do this. Stealing from the bank is like stealing from your own family."

Danny drained his glass. "Are you sure it's an inside job?"

"No, but it's a definite possibility. Mr. Weber won't face it, so I have to."

Elizabeth Hall picked up her glass and took a long drink.

Danny kissed his mother and left the room.

He went to his room and began to clean up. Suddenly he stopped, lost in thought. He sat down at his computer. He turned on his modem, then typed furiously for several minutes. He stopped typing just as suddenly. He flopped onto his bed and picked up his dog.

"There's no listing anywhere. It must be a private number only given to employees." He patted Hacker for several minutes while he thought.

His mother poked her head into the room. "This room is starting to look better already. It shouldn't take you long. Don't forget to do your homework. I'm going to take a shower. If the phone rings, please take a message."

"Sure, Mom." Danny continued to pat Hacker.

A few minutes later, Danny had an idea. When he heard the water running in the bathroom, he went downstairs to the living room. He opened his mother's desk drawer and shuffled through the papers quickly. Then he quietly closed the drawer and tiptoed up the stairs and back to his room. He sat down at the computer and started to type.

"OK, Hacker, we're on our way!"

# CHAPTER FOUR

When Danny slid into his seat on the bus the next morning, he wasn't his usual self. Even Jason noticed how quiet he was.

"Hi, Dan, you look awful. Didn't you sleep last night?"

Danny pushed the hair off his forehead. "No, I was up most of the night."

Jason jabbed Danny in the ribs. "Up all night studying, right?"

Danny laughed. "Right, studying. Actually, I was at the computer all night. I think I've found a way to save my mom's job."

"Wait a minute, Dan. Back up. What's going on?"

"Mom's got a problem at her bank — someone's been embezzling from client accounts, and they don't know who it is. I'm out to solve the problem."

And he told his friend of his plan, an

inspired idea that left Jason slightly bewildered.

"...and I'll set up a WATCHDOG subroutine, and as soon as he tries to transfer the funds from the corporation, I'll nail him."

Jason grabbed Danny's arm. They stood up and walked to the front of the bus. "Danny, this is totally bizarre. You aren't planning to try to catch this guy all by yourself, are you?"

"No, of course not. As soon as we trace the call, I'll notify the police. Only, you're right, I'm going to need some help."

Students pushed and shoved them to get off the bus.

They continued the conversation in front of the school. Danny's mind was full of ideas. He needed Jason. He had to convince him.

"Hold it. Don't look at me, Sherlock

Junior. You're the computer whiz!"

Danny looked straight at Jason. "I thought you were my friend."

Jason leaned against the door. "I am. Your best. That's why I can tell you this. You are crazy. Loco. Out of your mind. You can't be serious about trying this."

Danny grabbed Jason. "Why not?"

"I'll tell you why not. It's illegal, that's why not. You'd be guilty of the same thing as the thief—unauthorized access to a computer system. Even if you weren't accessing the system to steal from it, you'd still be in big trouble. And it could be dangerous. What if the thief caught you instead of the other way around? This person could be desperate enough to . . ."

"Don't say it. Don't even think it. I told you I'd be careful. You're beginning to sound just like my mom."

"You told her about this silly scheme?"

Danny put his hand on Jason's shoulder. "Now who's sounding crazy? I can't tell her until it's all over. She'd never agree to it. That's why I need help. I'll never be able to stay up around the clock. And I'll need some help from the phone company."

Jason smiled. "And that's where I fit in ... it wouldn't have anything to do with my brother Mike working at the phone company, would it?" He looked up to the sky. "Why me?"

"Hey, would you call Mike? Please? You like my mom. You could help her save her job."

Jason sighed. "OK. You talked me into it. I'll call Mike after school. Hey, we'd better get inside. The bell's going to ring any minute."

"Do you think your parents would let you spend the weekend at my house?" Danny asked.

The two boys walked down the hall to their lockers.

Jason stopped in mid-combination and spun around to face Danny. "Hold it right there. I've got a date with Lauren tonight!"

Danny slowly turned the dial on his lock. "OK, I'll ask Paul."

Jason opened his locker and took out his books. "Paul, that creep? Why him?"

"Because he's a hacker, too, and he probably won't be too busy—like some people."

Jason slammed his locker shut.

"That's unfair—what a thing to say!"

Then he calmed down and thought about how he could get around his date with Lauren.

"OK, OK, you win. I'll take Lauren to the early show and come right over. Thanks for wrecking my night, friend. So . . . I guess I'll see you tonight."

Danny took out his books and closed his locker gingerly. For some strange reason, nothing fell on him today.

## CHAPTER FIVE

Danny had already been at the computer for several hours when Jason arrived.

Jason stepped over piles of disks and papers to get to Danny.

"Hi, Dan, how's it going?"

Danny didn't look up from the keyboard. "Terrible. What made me think I could do this? It'll take years to hack out. There must be millions of possible combinations."

Picking up some of the papers from the chair and putting them on Danny's desk, Jason sat down. There was a slight smudge of lipstick on his left cheek, but Danny didn't say anything.

"Don't give up, Dan. I know you can do it. You didn't think you could pass your history test, either, but you did it. Keep at it. It's a perfect way to set a trap. Can you imagine your mom's face if we manage to pull it off! Imagine her telling her boss that her son cracked the case and saved the bank!"

Danny looked up from the keyboard and stared at Jason.

"Picture the thief's face when he finds out the company he's stealing from doesn't exist. Can you imagine what he'll say when the cops tell him the trap was set by a couple of teenage hackers!"

Jason jumped up from his seat. He was getting a little carried away, thought Danny, who still couldn't get a word in.

"And wait until the kids at school hear about this! Michelle will certainly know who you are. And it wouldn't hurt my standing with Lauren either."

Danny eyed the lipstick smudge again. Jason's standing with Lauren was OK.

Danny got back to the keyboard. "What are we waiting for? Let's get back to work. We only have until Monday morning to catch this creep."

By 3 A.M. the boys had reached the end of their patience. Mrs. Hall had come in twice to check on things, but it was a Friday night and she wasn't about to question them while the computer was being used. Jason finally conked out on Danny's bed, with Hacker asleep at his feet, but Danny was too keyed up to sleep, and he kept plugging away at the computer. By 4 A.M. he'd had enough. He was surrounded by empty soda cans and candy wrappers. He picked up Hacker. She let out an annoyed yelp, which woke Jason.

"What gives, Dan?"

"It's no use, I can't do it. I can't access the system. The embezzler hacked his way in, but I can't."

"You don't know how long it took. He could have been at it for months," said Jason.

"That's just it. We don't have unlimited

time. The only way to set up the WATCHDOG this weekend is to use my mom's name and password."

"Would she give it to you?" asked Jason.

Danny paced up and down the room.

"I don't dare ask her. If I log on using her name and password, and we don't catch this guy, everyone will think my mom's the embezzler. She could go to jail. Even if she can prove she's not the thief, and they find out she let me use her password, she could still lose her job for allowing unauthorized use of the system. Either way, it's bad news."

Danny took a long gulp from the can in his hand.

"But that's only if we fail," said Jason. "And if we stand by and do nothing, she'll lose her job when the bank goes out of business. We're running out of time. Monday morning her boss will go to the police, and we lose our chance to try the plan. I say we have to take the risk."

Danny stopped pacing. "But I can't involve Mom. I'll have to swipe her password. That way, if the plan doesn't work, she won't be involved."

"Do you know where she keeps it?"

Danny thought for a minute. "No, but there are only two places in the house she would. Her briefcase or her desk. Let's try the desk first."

The boys tiptoed down the steps to the living room. They opened one drawer at a time, careful not to make any noise. They each took a stack of papers and sat down on the floor. They went through each pile carefully, examining every paper. No luck.

"We'll have to try her briefcase," said Danny.

"Where's that?"

"In her room. On the chair next to

her bed."

"I was afraid of that," said Jason.

Quietly, they put the papers back in the drawers and made their way back up the stairs.

"Wait in my room," whispered Danny. "No sense both of us getting caught."

Danny opened his mother's door slowly.

He inched his way into the room, careful not to bump into anything. His mother was sleeping soundly, her breathing soft.

Danny suddenly realized how pretty his mom looked. Next to Jason, she was probably his best friend. Very slowly, he opened the briefcase and examined the papers. Then, very quietly, he put everything back the way it was and closed the case. Then he crept out of the room and carefully shut the door behind him.

"Did you get it?" whispered Jason.

Danny nodded.

"Where? Let me see." said Jason.

Danny pointed to his head and sat down at the computer.

An hour later, everything was all set up. Danny got up from his chair and stretched.

"I opened a new account for a phony corporation. I backdated it to Friday, just before closing time, so it will look like the account was opened at the bank.

Sooner or later, that greedy thief will snap at the bait. Then, the computer will beep, alerting us to the transaction. Then all we have to do is call Mike to trace the call, and WHAM, the trap will clang shut. We'll have him."

Jason slapped Danny on the back. "And we'll be heroes!"

# CHAPTER SIX

All day Saturday, the boys kept a stake-out in Danny's room. Combat ready, like soldiers on red alert, they jumped at every noise.

Danny's mother had gone to play golf for the day, although she said her handicap would suffer because she had too much on her mind.

By the end of the day, the boys were pretty discouraged.

"Maybe the thief gave up and left town," said Danny.

Jason disagreed. "That thief is still out there—we just have to be patient. I'll stand guard—you catch a nap."

"OK, just a short nap. Then I'll take over while you sleep."

Danny stretched out on his bed, exhausted. The events of the past few days had finally caught up with him. He dreamed about police detectives on a stake-out, spies listening to wiretaps, and rescuing Michelle from a band of rebels. He had her in his arms and was just about to lay one of the world's best kisses on her lips when he was shaken awake.

It was Jason. "No action," he said.

Danny looked at the clock. He had slept three hours.

"I don't think it's going to work," said Danny. The thief is too smart. He's lying low until things quiet down. I think my mom's right about it being an inside job. The embezzler knows the bank's suspicious. I think we should close down the WATCHDOG and remove all traces of my mom's access to the system."

"I think we should hold out until tomorrow night," said Jason. "If it's an inside job, the thief will feel safe until Monday morning. Nobody at the bank knows what we're doing. I've only told Mike, and he told two friends at the phone company so we'd have all the shifts covered. You haven't told anyone, have you?"

"No," said Danny. "Not even my mother."

A few hours later, it happened. Jason was asleep on Danny's bed with Hacker at his feet. It was Danny's watch. He was leaning back in his chair, his feet up on the desk, reading a few pages of Stephen King's *The Shining*, when the computer beeped. He jumped up, threw the book at the sleeping Jason and raced down the stairs to the kitchen phone.

His fingers trembled as he dialed Mike's number. Mike picked up on the first ring. Danny said only one word: "Now." He held on, pacing the kitchen floor, while Mike traced the call and notified the police. It was the longest minute of his life. When he hung up the phone, his body felt limp as the importance of what had just happened finally sunk in. The next minute he was riding high, the adrenalin was pumping. They'd done it. He raced up the stairs, yelling.

Jason, still rubbing tired eyes, met him at the door of the bedroom.

"Jason, we've got him! It worked. It really worked."

"Are you kidding? You mean we really did it?"

Hacker jumped off the bed and started barking.

"I'd better go tell my mom."

"Tell me what?" Mrs. Hall stood in the doorway. "What on earth are you yelling about? Do you have any idea what time it is?"

"I got him. I mean we got him. Me and Jason. I mean Jason and I. Whatever. Anyway we got him."

Mrs. Hall faced Danny.

"Slow down, I'm not following you.
What did you get?"

Danny took a deep breath. "Not what!
Who! We got him."

Mrs. Hall still looked puzzled.

Danny started again. "The thief. The bank thief."

A half-smile crossed Mrs. Hall's face. "Are you kidding? If this is some kind of joke, Danny, it's not at all funny."

Danny gave his mom a quick hug. "I'm serious. Mike's already called the police."

Mrs. Hall looked puzzled again. "But how? Who's Mike? You better explain yourself, Danny Hall!"

Danny grinned. "It's a long story but it's OK."

Mrs. Hall seemed relieved. "All I know is that you and Jason have been holed up here all weekend. I figured it was another one of your computer projects."

Danny's grin spread even wider. "Yeah, a computer project. My best one yet. We set a trap for the embezzler. I accessed the bank's files and opened an account for a phony corporation. Then after we set the trap, we just sat back and waited. That was the hard part. But sure enough, that greedy creep couldn't resist the new account."

Danny was racing.

"Slow down, slow down, let me get it all in," said his mom, having to sit down with the sheer excitement of the moment.

"Just a little while ago, the thief transferred a hundred dollars from the Tritech Electronics Corporation. With some help from Jason's brother Mike at the phone company, we traced the number. See, the bank has about twenty phone lines connected to the system. But only two of them were in use just now—mine and the thief's. Since Mike already knew my number, the other one had to be the embezzler. While I held on, he put a trace on that one and called the police. The police are on their way to a house on Park Street right now. Can you take me and Jason to the police station? We just gotta be there when they bring this guy in."

Mrs. Hall grabbed Danny in a bear hug. "You're amazing."

"I know."

"But how did you access the bank's files?"

"Don't be mad. When I couldn't hack out the codes, I used your name and password to enter the system. I took your password out of your briefcase while you were sleeping."

Mrs. Hall sat down again. "Oh, Danny, do you have any idea what you've done? We both may be in a lot of trouble! You broke the law. If you aren't right, we'll be in a fine pickle. Well, what's done is done. I'd better call Mr. Weber. He'll want to be there, too."

## CHAPTER SEVEN

It was 3:15 A.M. when the police car pulled up in front of 185 Park Street. No siren, no lights, no noise.

Two officers got out of the car. Officers Harvey Cameron and Jane Green made their way up to the house. There was a light on somewhere at the back of the house.

Officer Cameron rang the bell.

No response from inside the house.

"Let's take a look around," he said.

"Over here," shouted Officer Cameron. "The back door is wide open."

Officer Green shone her flashlight around the yard.

They could just make out a thin figure in jeans and a sweatshirt climbing over the back fence.

"There goes our suspect," said Officer Cameron.

The police officers ran across the yard.

"Hey, you! Stop right there! Police!" yelled Officer Green.

They climbed the fence in time to see their suspect round the corner and head down the block. The shadowy figure crossed through yards, over fences, and through bushes, staying just enough ahead to be seen—yet just out of reach. If not for bumping into a trash can and sprawling out on the pavement, the suspect might have made a clean getaway.

Officer Cameron snapped on the handcuffs. "You have the right to remain silent but anything you say..."

When Mrs. Hall and the two boys entered the police station, Mr. Weber was already there. He walked over to greet them.

"So these are the two heroes!"

"Er...yes, you already know my son, Daniel," said Mrs. Hall. "This is his friend, Jason Miller."

Everyone shook hands.

There was an air of excitement in the office.

"Looks like we have to sit and wait. All I can say is, well done, boys, and I hope the villain is caught. We should know soon enough."

Danny nodded. "Then you're not going to send me to jail for swiping the codes and accessing the bank's files?"

"Send you to jail? Oh no. If you'd only asked me, I would have GIVEN you MY password."

Danny uttered a sigh of relief. "I couldn't have done it without Jason, and his brother Mike and some of Mike's friends at the phone company."

The bank manager smiled at the two boys and then at Mrs. Hall.

"When I arrived, they had sent some officers to Park Street," said Mr. Weber. "They've arrested someone. I've been filling out papers since I got here. It looks like they've got a strong case. Caught the thief red-handed."

Mrs. Hall sat down beside her boss. "Did they say who it was?" she asked.

"No, no one's talking. But I guess we'll know soon enough."

When officers Cameron and Green arrived with the thief, Mr. Weber and Mrs. Hall jumped up from the bench. Mr. Weber gasped.

"I don't believe it. Sara Gordon, of all people."

Sara Gordon looked right at Mr. Weber.

"I don't seem the type, do I. Think I don't know anything about computers? Do you think I'm only good enough to make your coffee and take notes?"

Mr. Weber shook his head. "But after all these years? Doesn't loyalty mean anything? Haven't I treated you fairly? Haven't I paid you well?"

Sara Gordon laughed. "Sure, for a secretary. I happen to have a brain, in case you haven't noticed. Well, now everyone will notice. I loved watching you squirm. I loved every minute of your frantic meetings where you watched the bank going under while I sat there calmly taking notes. I loved typing the memos to your executives as you puzzled over this sophisticated thief who was stealing you blind—this clever embezzler who was right under your nose all the time. But I was invisible. All secretaries are invisible, aren't they? Just type this letter, Sara, get the phone, Sara, send this package, Sara, make some coffee, Sara, make some more coffee, Sara, make lots of coffee, Sara..."

She was still babbling as the officers led her away to be fingerprinted.

Mr. Warren rubbed his forehead. "I just can't believe it. I always trusted her. She was so efficient. She never complained. How was I to know she was unhappy? Secretaries were always happy to be secretaries. Now, I don't know any more..."

Mrs. Hall put a comforting arm on his shoulder. "You've been under quite a strain. Try to relax."

A police officer came over to them. "Can I get you folks anything? Some coffee, perhaps?"

Mr. Weber put his hand over his face.

# CHAPTER EIGHT

When Danny dashed out of his front door on Monday morning, the bus was waiting on the corner with the motor running.

There was a rousing cheer as he got on the bus.

He had to break through a crowd of kids surrounding Jason to get to his seat. Paul was holding a morning newspaper. Pictures of Danny and Jason were on the front page. The headline read: LOCAL STUDENTS FOIL THIEF

Paul was reading the article out loud. "...Daniel Hall and Jason Miller will be honored at a ceremony at City Hall this Saturday at 2 P.M. At that time, they will receive medals from the mayor and generous scholarship awards from Columbia Bank."

Lauren leaned over the seat, poking her head between her two friends.

"How does it feel to be heroes, guys?"

"Great," said Jason. "Let me tell you all about it after school—at Coco's Cafe."

Lauren smiled and gave him a peck on the cheek. "Sure, I'd love to hear all the exciting details."

When the bus pulled up in front of the school, Michelle was waiting with a group of her friends.

Everyone had heard about the incident.

Danny jumped down from the bus and walked over to her. "Hi, Michelle, can I walk you to class?"

"I thought you'd never ask," she said.